A modern approach

Reading and writing should flow through the natural activities and interests of the child. The next most important aid is a series of books designed to stimulate and interest him and to give daily practice at the right level.

Educational experts from five Caribbean countries have co-operated with the author to design and produce this Ladybird Sunstart Reading Scheme. Their work has been influenced by (a) the widely accepted piece of research *Key Words to Literacy*[1], a word list which is adapted here for tropical countries and used to accelerate learning in the early stages; and (b) the work of Dr. Dennis Craig[2] of the School of Education, U.W.I., and other specialists who have carried out research in areas where the English language is being ung children whose natural spe ring school is a patois or dialect der-ably from standard English.

[1] *'Key Words to Literacy' by J. McNall published by The Schoolmaster Publi Derbyshire House, Kettering, Northant*

[2] *'An experiment in teaching English' by Caribbean Universities Press, also 'To), Journal of the Ministry of Education, Jamaica.*

THE LADYBIRD SUNSTART READING SCHEME will consist of six books and three workbooks. These are graded and written with a controlled vocabulary and plentiful repetition. They are fully illustrated.

Book 1 'Lucky dip' (for beginners) is followed by Book 2 'On the beach'. Workbook A is parallel to these and covers the vocabulary of both books. The workbook reinforces the words learned in the readers, teaches handwriting and introduces phonic training.

Book 3 'The kite' and Book 4 'Animals, birds and fish' follow Books 1 and 2, and are supported by Workbook B. This reinforces the vocabulary of Books 3 and 4 and again contains handwriting exercises and phonic training.

Book 5 'I wish' and Book 6 'Guess what?' with Workbook C complete the scheme.

The illustrated handbook for parents and teachers is entitled 'A Guide to the Teaching of Reading'.

For classroom use there are two boxes of large flash cards which cover the first three books, and ten wall pictures with matching sentence strips.

BOOK 5

The Ladybird SUNSTART Reading Scheme
(a 'Key Words' Reading Scheme)

I wish

by W. MURRAY
with illustrations by MARTIN AITCHISON

Publishers: Ladybird Books Ltd . Loughborough
in collaboration with Longman Caribbean Ltd
© Ladybird Books Ltd 1975
Printed in England

The rain comes

These boys and girls have been playing in the sun, but the rain has come. They all run to shelter from the rain.

When the rain stops they will go from the shelter to play again. But the rain goes on for a long time.

"What can we do?" one girl asks.

"We can play something under here," another girl says.

"I know," calls out a big boy. "I know what to do – we can play I WISH!"

"Yes," say some of the others. "Let's play I WISH!"

"How do we play that?" asks a little girl.

The others tell her. "You just tell everyone what you want to be or what you want to do, or where you want to go."

"I will go first!" calls out a little boy. "I know just what I want to be. I'll tell you!"

INDEX

PRINTED IN GREAT BRITAIN AT
THE PRESS OF THE PUBLISHERS

The giant

"Yes, let him go first," says the big boy. He helps the small boy up, so that the others can see him.

All the children look at the little boy as he talks.

"I don't want to be little," the boy says. "I don't like being small. I want to be big. I want to be very big. My wish is to be a giant. Yes, that's it. I want to be a giant!"

The little boy closes his eyes. "When I close my eyes I can see it," he says. "I am big now! I am very big! I am as big as a tree! I am a giant!

"I am very strong now. I am so strong that I can hold one of you up in one of my hands, and another of you in the other. I like being a giant! But I am a kind giant. I don't want to hurt people. I want to help everyone."

The giant

The little boy who wishes to be a giant goes on talking. He closes his eyes again.

"I can see a mountain," he says. "Some people are on the mountain. They are in danger. It is dangerous for them but there is no danger for me, as I am so big and strong.

"The people have climbed up the mountain but now they can't climb down. They don't know what to do. They are afraid. I am not afraid and I know how to save them.

" 'Don't be afraid,' I say to the people. 'I am going to save you. I will get you down from the mountain. Just climb on to my hand and hold on. There is no danger now.' "

The people are not afraid of the giant. They see that he is kind and that he can save them. When they climb on to his hand they are saved. They thank the giant very much for saving them.

The giant

This little boy's name is Sam. He is the one who wants to be a giant. Sam says that he has one more adventure to tell the others. It is an adventure about danger at sea.

He says that a boy and girl are at sea in a small boat. Sam the giant is on the shore. There is no rain, but the wind makes the sea rough.

Then the wind is very strong and the sea more and more rough. It is so rough that the children in the boat are in danger. They are afraid.

The girl falls out of the boat. As she falls she calls, "Help! Help!"

Sam hears her when she calls. He comes from the shore just in time to lift the girl out of the water. He lifts her with one hand. With his other hand he lifts the boat from the sea on to the shore.

The boy falls out of the boat on to the shore but he is not hurt.

The magic carpet

"My turn," says a girl named Pam. "It's my turn now. I'll close my eyes to have my wish and then tell you about it."

Pam says, "I have a magic carpet. I just sit on my magic carpet and float through the air. There's no danger on my magic carpet. I can't fall off. I float where I want to go and then float back here again.

"Now I want to go to Africa to see the large animals there. Africa is very far away but on my magic carpet it will take very little time to get there. I'll take my brother with me."

Pam goes on, "We are over Africa now. We can see some very large animals as we look down. They don't run away. My brother and I like all animals and we don't want to catch them."

"Look out, or some of them will catch you !" calls out little Sam.

13

The magic carpet

The wonderful magic carpet floats high in the air over the countries of Africa. There is no wind where they are.

There is much to see in Africa, but before long the magic carpet moves on. It goes very quickly over a great sea.

Then the brother and sister look down on the shores of another great country. It is India. There are high mountains there. India is another very beautiful country. Many, many people live in Africa and India.

"I like being up here," says Pam to her brother. "It makes me want to read about these wonderful countries and to learn more about them and their peoples. Are you afraid up here?"

"No, I'm not afraid at all," says the boy to his sister. "I want to go on and on. What a wonderful adventure to have!"

The magic carpet

On goes the magic carpet. It comes to the great land of China. China is another wonderful country where very many people live. Everyone knows a little about China, but not many people have been there.

The Great Wall of China is the first thing Pam and her brother see. It is very old and no other wall in the world is so large, so long and so strong. As they look down, the brother and sister can see people walking along the Great Wall.

On they go into China and then they see a kind of Carnival. Many people are in it. Some dance as they go along. Most are dressed in beautiful colours. Some are in what looks like a very large snake or caterpillar. This moves along with the people. It has a big head and some wings. It is a dragon.

"What a big caterpillar!" says the boy to his sister.

"No, it is not a caterpillar, it must be a dragon!" says Pam.

17

The magic carpet

"I want to go to a place called Disneyland," says Pam. "Disneyland is an amusement park in America," she tells her brother.

When the magic carpet knows Pam's wish it takes them quickly to America and stops over the amusement park called Disneyland.

Disneyland is for children but many men and women go there. People come to America from all over the world to see it. No other amusement park in the world is as large as this one.

They look down at the children. Many are with their parents. Parents and children all look happy.

"I wish we were down there with them," says Pam. As she says this, the magic carpet floats down into the amusement park so that they can get off. It is a big place in the park called Adventureland.

Pam and her brother play with other children in Adventureland and have a happy time. Then they get on the magic carpet and go back home.

By rocket to the moon

The big boy called Ben says that it is his turn for a wish.

"I don't want a magic carpet," he says. "I want a rocket. I want to go to the moon. Yes, my wish is to go in a rocket to the moon.

"I'll take little Sam with me. We'll be like the men from America who went to the moon. They went in a rocket. I'll tell you what I think it will be like.

"We are ready now, and the rocket is ready. Ready for lift-off. Come on, Sam, you get in first and we'll go. We'll soon be there."

In Ben's wish, the rocket takes off and is soon high in the air. It is on its way to the moon with Ben and Sam. They think that it is the most wonderful adventure to have. They are going away from this world to the moon and back.

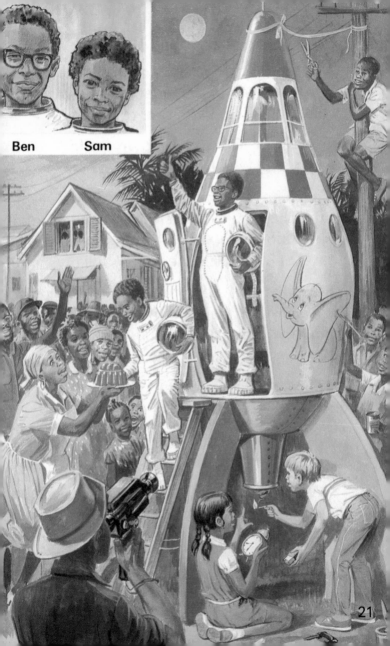

Ben   Sam

21

By rocket to the moon

Ben and Sam look out of the rocket as it goes on its way to the moon. They look back at the earth. The earth is far away now.

Ben says, "There is our own world. I think it's beautiful when you see it from here."

They can see many of the countries of the earth. They look for their own country, and Africa and India. Ben sees China and tells Sam that he can see the Great Wall of China.

Then the two boys turn to look the other way. They look at the moon. It is very big to them now. They can see high mountains on the moon.

"There will be no water, no people and no animals there," says Ben.

"And no trees and no flowers," says little Sam. "We will be on our own."

"We must get ready," Ben says. "We will be there soon. Just think, we are going to walk on the moon!"

23

By rocket to the moon

The rocket lands on the moon, and Ben and Sam climb out.

They know that no one lives on the moon because there is no air or water there. All of us must have air and water to live. If we go to the moon we must take our own air and water with us.

As there is no air or water on the moon there is no rain and no wind.

First the boys walk about. They soon learn to do this. Then they find that they can jump high. This is because the moon is not as large as the earth. The small moon does not pull down as hard as the big earth when they jump.

They go to see some of the mountains of the moon. Then they come to the place where the Americans were. They see the American flag and the other things that the first men on the moon left when they went there.

By rocket to the moon

Sam and Ben like being on the moon. They look at the flag and the other things left by the Americans.

Sam asks, "Do the Americans own the moon?"

"No," says Ben. "No country owns the moon. This flag means that the Americans were here."

"We are here," says Sam. "Can't we put up a flag?"

"We can't put one here because we have no flag with us," says Ben.

Sam says, "Can't we make a flag? We left some things in the rocket."

"Let's go back to the rocket and see if we can make a flag," says Ben.

The two boys look in the rocket for something like a flag. "How about this?" asks Sam.

"Yes," says Ben. "That will do. Come on, let's put it up." They put their flag by the American one.

"That means that Sam and Ben were here," says Sam. "Now we have to get back home."

They get into the rocket and are soon on their way back to earth.

The bottom of the deep sea

This girl's wish is to walk at the bottom of the deep sea. She wants to see what it is like very deep down under the water, away from the sun.

She sees large and small fish of many kinds down there. Some she has seen before, when she went to an Aquarium, but there are a great many others to be seen in the deep sea. Many of them have beautiful colours.

The girl doesn't want to catch anything. She just wants to look at the fish and the other things that live at the bottom or near the bottom of the sea.

She finds that there are mountains under the sea, as there are on land. She does not go near anything that looks dark or dangerous.

She thinks that the world under the sea is as wonderful as the one on earth where she lives.

The bottom of the deep sea

The girl knows that there are sunken ships at the bottom of the sea, but she has not seen a sunken ship before. Now she sees a large and very old sunken ship at the bottom of the sea.

It does not look dangerous so she swims near to look at it, and then swims inside.

She can see that there were no people on the ship when it went down. It looks as if the men on it had no time to take anything away from the ship before they left it.

The girl sees a large box of treasure. She thinks, "Why – it's a treasure ship! I must look at the treasure." She plays with some of the things in the treasure box.

Then something that looks dangerous comes inside where she is, so she swims away quickly from the sunken ship.

She swims away and finds that she has come back to the other children. Her wish is over. She has had her turn.

Fun on the ice

A girl called Pat talks to the others about her wish. Pat says, "My wish is to go to a cold country where there is a lot of ice.

"We know what ice is," she goes on. "We can make it here and many people use it in the house or at work. But in some countries it is so cold that the rain comes down as ice. The rain turns into ice on the way down through the air as it falls.

"In these cold countries water outside the house can turn into ice. Ice is hard and cold but you can use it to have lots of fun.

"You can skate on it, or slide on it. It is fun to go fast when you skate or slide."

In her wish Pat has lots of fun with other children on the ice. They slide and skate for a long time. Some fall over but they are not hurt.

Fun with snow

There is snow now. Lots of cold snow floats down through the air and covers the land like a white carpet. It covers the houses and the trees and falls on the people as they walk about outside.

The children have fun in the snow. As the snow covers their slide on the ice, they can't use it to skate, so they make a ball out of the snow and push it along. This snowball gets bigger and bigger as they push it.

Then they make a man out of some snow.
The snowman is large and they put a hat on it.
They throw snowballs at the snowman and
throw snowballs at one another.

Some children use skis. On these skis they
can learn to move quickly over the snow. They
can jump on skis. Pat can ski jump from a high
place. She flies through the air on her skis to
land on the snow at the bottom.

The cricket test match

"Cricket," says the boy with the bat. "My wish is about cricket! I wish I could play for my country at cricket all over the world. I wish I could be playing now!" He closes his eyes to help him to see this.

When one country plays another at cricket it is called a test match. It is a test match now. Many people have come to see this test match. They sit in the sun and look at the players as they bat and bowl for their country.

One player bowls the ball to the other with the bat. The one with the bat hits the ball. He hits it high in the air. Another player runs to catch the ball as it comes down. He catches it and the man with the bat is out. He has been caught out.

Now it is the turn of our boy. It is his turn to bat. He bats for a long time. He hits the ball hard, many times, and makes a lot of runs.

The test match

The cricket test match goes on all day. This is the last day of play. The sun is out and it is hot. Many people have come on this last day to see which country will win.

Our boy has had his turn with the bat. He got a lot of runs and then was run out.

The players of the other country now go in to bat. One big man plays very well. Again and again he hits the ball a long way to make many runs.

The men who bowl can't get him out. They bowl as fast as they can but he just hits the ball away to make more runs.

If he goes on like this he could soon win this test match for his country. He is a wonderful player.

Then the men throw the ball to our boy and tell him to bowl. He bowls very well and at last gets the big man out. Our boy goes on to win the test match for his country.

The Olympic Games

This little girl's name is Ann. Ann was always good at games and good at running. As a very small girl she was always playing games with bigger children and running races with them. Ann could always win the races.

She is bigger now, but not so very big, and she has her wish. The wish is to run for her country at the World Olympic Games.

As you know, there are men and women from many countries who come to the Olympic Games. They come from all over the world.

The Olympic Games are not for children, but our little girl, Ann, has had her magic wish and she is running there. She is the one girl who runs in the race. Her magic wish is to run so well that she wins her race.

She does run very fast and comes in first. Ann wins for her country at the World Olympic Games. This is her big day!

104

The Olympic Games

If you win your race at the Olympic Games you get a gold medal. You can keep the medal. Ann's wish was to win an Olympic gold medal and she has done it. She came first in her race.

Ann goes up to get her gold medal now. Two women in the race have medals as well as Ann, but theirs are not gold. The medal which is gold is for the one who came first.

The band plays as the medals are put on. The people there say, "Good girl, well done!" and Ann looks very happy.

There is some amusement as the girl is so small. The medal looks big on her.

Ann knows that the race for the gold medal is in her magic wish. But she thinks that when she grows up she will come again to the Olympic Games to run for her country. Then she will win an Olympic gold medal to keep.

On the island

Another boy talks about a wish. He wants an island of his own.

He says, "If I had an island of my own my friends and I could have a lot of fun on it. There would be no parents there." Then, as he talks, he thinks he is there. Now he can see his own island in the sun. He thinks that he is on it with his friends.

He goes on, "My friends and I can swim in the sea or play cricket on the sand as long as we like. We can make a raft and have fun with that.

"We can make our own house. If it rains we can play in it.

"There is a lot to do. We can look for treasure, and have adventures. We can find things to eat or look at animals, birds, fish and insects.

"My friends and I have no work to do and we are happy all the time on my island."

On the island

There are girls on the island as well as boys. One of the girls is very good at singing. She wants to sing a song to her friends now. They know that she is a good singer and they tell her to go on.

She sings a happy song about the children there and about the games which they like to play. She makes up the song as she goes along.

All the children's wishes come into the song. She sings of the giant and the magic carpet, the moon rocket, treasure in the sea and the ice and snow. She tells of the cricket match, the Olympic Games and the girl with her gold medal.

She gets the others to sing and then they dance. They are all very happy.

The girl tells the other children that she wants to be a singer when she grows up.

The rain stops

A boy calls out, "My wish has just come true! I have been wishing and wishing that the rain would stop, and now it has! Look, the sun is out! Let's go!"

The children run out from their shelter. They stop wishing and soon are playing cricket and other games in the sun.

There is a slide there, and some of the boys and girls go on that. Ann, who is good at running, gets some of her friends to run races with her.

Little Sam's ball is in a tree. He throws things at it to get it down.

"Do wishes come true?" asks one little girl.

"I wish they would," says her sister.

"I think that they come true sometimes," says another little girl.

A boy near them says, "Sometimes a wish comes true when you work for it. If you work very hard for what you want, sometimes you get it."

49

Read the words with the help of the pictures.
Then cover the pictures and read the words.

1 She is inside the shelter and he is outside.
2 He asks his parents which one he can keep.
3 The sun makes everything grow.
4 Which is bigger, the earth or the moon?
5 Would you like to be a singer?
6 The sea is rough because the wind is strong.
7 She uses the last one.
8 The two children make a dragon.
9 He swims near a sunken ship.
10 The snow came and covered the house.
11 They throw snowballs at the snowman.
12 He has had his wish.
13 The players bat and bowl.
14 Always keep away from danger.
15 This girl is good at running.
16 This is a gold medal.

Words new to the series used in this book

Total number of words 124